Rabbi Rocketpower
AND
The Mystery
OF THE
Missing Menorahs -
A Hanukkah Humdinger!

To Eli,
Enjoy!
Rabbi Sun Abramson

Written by
Rabbi Susan Abramson
AND Aaron Dvorkin

Illustrated by
Ariel DiOrio

In loving memory

of

"Dad"

ABOUT THE AUTHORS

Rabbi Susan Abramson is a graduate of Brandeis University and Hebrew Union College – Jewish Institute of Religion.

She has been the rabbi of Temple Shalom Emeth in Burlington, Massachusetts since 1984.

Aaron Dvorkin, her son, is a middle school student.

ABOUT THE ILLUSTRATOR

Ariel DiOrio is a senior in high school.   She plans to pursue a career in art.

CONTENTS

INTRODUCTION
MEET THE MENSCHES

Not so long ago...

in a place not too far from here...

lived a mom...

a dad...

a boy...

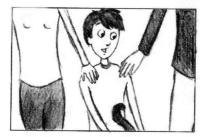

and a cat.

If you met them, you would never notice anything unusual. But for those in the know, this was one very unique family.

You see, the mom was not only a mom. She was a *rabbi*. And she wasn't only a rabbi. She was a rabbi with super powers.

Everyone knew her as Rabbi Beatrice Ann Mensch (B.A. *Mensch* for short). But before you could say "*Shma Yisrael*," she could transform herself into the courageous, all powerful, all knowing Rabbi Rocketpower … able to wipe out evil wherever she found it, able to make bad guys turn good with a flick of her mighty *yad*, able to make peace when there was war with a blast from her trusty *shofar*. Whenever she blasted off on one of her missions, she would shout "*Oy Vay*! Up, up and away!"

The dad was no ordinary dad. He was a brilliant, multilingual computer expert, able to find any information on his trusty secret supercomputer. No matter what you needed to know, no matter what language it was in, he could find it before you could type: www.helpmefindthisinformation.com.

And Aaron was no ordinary boy. He could spot trouble a mile away, smell a rat, sniff a skunk… well, you get the idea.

He was always the first to notice when something

was not so *kosher*. He
was his mother's trusty
right-hand boy. No one
knew it, but he was a
Super-Boy-in-Training.

Last, but not least, was their crazy cat Purr. She looked
like an ordinary black cat with white paws and a white
stripe running down her stomach. But, in fact, she was the
only cat on earth who could talk. And most of the time,
what she said was not very nice.

Blow it out your ear, nincompoop!

The Mensch family thought they had adopted a cute little kitten when they went to the local animal shelter.

Hey! Put me down you birdbrains!

But after they brought Purr home, she informed them that her full name was "Purreneal Pest" and that she was actually an alien from the planet *P.I.A.,* which stands for "Pain In the Asteroid."

Yum...tasty!

She preferred spending her days chasing her tail, trying to catch bugs on the ceiling, chewing up plants and drinking out of the toilet.

Purr often referred to the members of her new family as "bub," "bubba," or "buster."

She was always telling them to mind their own business or to go stuff it in a *matzah ball*. But when the family was busy fighting evil, she did condescend to help out.

Purr! We need your help!

Whatever, bubba.

Uch. This is so annoying.

Unfortunately, trouble was brewing while the Mensches were about to celebrate one of Aaron's favorite Jewish holidays.

Who was causing the problem this time? Monsters? Kookie clowns from outer space? Funny Fruitanians on a field trip from the planet Pun? A boastful *blintz* who wanted to rule the world? Morphing matzah on  a misguided mission? Roving rodents who ran out of gas?

Get set for a hilarious, out-of-this-world, action-packed adventure.

Oy Vay! Up, up and away!

~ ~ ~ ~ ~

CHAPTER ONE
PURR'S FIRST HANUKKAH

Aaron couldn't wait to get home from school. "Purr!" he called excitedly as he ran into the house, "Guess what tonight is?"

"Don't yell! Can't you see I'm sleeping, bubble brain?" whined Purr. She reluctantly opened one eye from her favorite napping position, curled up in a ball on top of the living room couch. "I know. It's 'Go Soak Your Head in a Fishbowl Night.' "

"Purr," Aaron exclaimed. "It's going to be your very first *Hanukkah!*"

"Hanukkah, shmanukkah," yawned Purr. "Wake me up when it's over."

"You don't even know what Hanukkah is," Aaron insisted. "First of all, it lasts for eight days."

"Eight days!" she groaned, rolling onto her back and sticking her paws in the air. "This is going to be one long catnap."

"Second of all," Aaron continued, trying to ignore her, "We get to make delicious potato pancakes called *latkes* and jelly doughnuts called *sufganiot.*"

"Remind me to lick them when you're done," Purr smirked, rolling her eyes.

"Then we get to play *dreidel* with chocolate coins called *gelt*," said Aaron, trying to entice her. "I'll even let you borrow my favorite gold dreidel which always lands on the letter '*gimmel*.' Then you'll be able to take all the gelt in the pot."

"If it's not a pot full of catnip, I ain't interested, buster," Purr huffed.

Aaron wasn't about to give up. "Then we get to light the Hanukkah *menorah*. We even get to choose which color candle we want to put in each candle holder."

"Don't you know I prefer it when it's dark?" she snickered, starting to get really annoyed.

"Purr, I bet if you knew why we celebrate Hanukkah, you'd really like it," Aaron insisted, trying to think of a way to keep her interested.

"Tell someone who cares." Purr jumped off the couch, stuck her nose in the air and pranced toward the door.

"It's about a really bad cat named *Antiochus*," Aaron added quickly. He knew that she liked stories about bad guys. "Antiochus made the Jews leave their holy Temple in Jerusalem. Then he and his army destroyed all of the beautiful things inside."

"Really?" Purr asked from the doorway.

Aaron knew he had her attention and continued. "Antiochus sent his army all over Israel to tell the Jews to stop being Jewish and to bow down to his idols. But when they got to a town called *Modiin*, Judah and the

Maccabees wouldn't bow down and they began to fight for their rights."

"I always love a good fight!" said Purr. "Keep going."

"Well, after a long time, the Maccabees and their followers beat Antiochus's army and got back their holy Temple. After they cleaned it up, some people say they lit a little jar of oil which miraculously burned for eight days.

"Others say after they cleaned up the temple, the Jews celebrated *Sukkot* for eight days, since that was their most important holiday.

"Either way, that's why we celebrate for eight days. That's why we eat food fried in oil. That's why we call the holiday Hanukkah, because it means 'rededication' in Hebrew," Aaron explained. "Isn't that great?"

"I can't believe that dude Antiochus lost," Purr snorted. "There's no way I'm going to celebrate a holiday about that!"

"Oh Purr," called Aaron as she trotted out of the room. "I forgot to tell you the best part. We all get presents after we light the candles. And I got you something special!"

"We'll see how special it is, latke breath." Purr stuck her nose in the air and continued on her way.

Aaron knew that Purr was very hard to please. No matter what he gave her – a ball with a bell in the middle, a long piece of ribbon, a rubber mouse – she would play with it for two seconds, then say "big deal," and walk away insulted.

But this time, Aaron had found the perfect toy. It was a small fishing rod with a catnip-coated mouse at the end of a long string. Whenever you touched the mouse, it would say, "Ouch! That hurt!" Aaron was sure that Purr would be intrigued by a toy that talked back to her. He couldn't wait to see her get into an argument with it.

CHAPTER TWO
GOT MENORAHS?

Rabbi Mensch called from her study upstairs,
"Aaron, could you please take the menorah down
from the mantel and put it on the dining room table?
It's almost time to light the candles."

Aaron grabbed a chair, and brought it over to the
fireplace. He reached up over the wooden ledge and felt
around right in the middle where he knew the menorah
was always kept. But he couldn't find it!

He jumped off the chair and took a couple of steps back to see if someone had moved it slightly. But it wasn't on the mantel at all. He looked all over the living room, the dining room, the kitchen, even under his bed. It was nowhere to be found.

"Very funny, mom," he shouted, assuming his mother was playing a trick on him. "Where did you hide it?"

"What are you talking about?" she answered. "It's right where it always is."

"No it isn't!" Aaron insisted, starting to get upset.

At that moment, Purr walked by and Aaron guessed what must have happened. "Purr, can you give me back the menorah, please?"

"What would I do with some dumb old menorah?" she answered.

"That's not nice!" Aaron scolded.

Just then, the phone rang. It was Aaron's friend Adam from up the street. "What?" Aaron said, "You can't find your Hanukkah menorah either? I'll call you back in a second." Aaron ran to the stairs. "Mom! Our *hanukkiah* is missing and so is Adam's!"

"I'm sure they're somewhere," she yelled. "I'll help you look after I finish wrapping these presents."

The phone rang again. "No, we don't have an extra menorah," he told Zoe, who lived around the corner. "You can't find yours either?"

Suddenly a dazzling bright light beamed through the kitchen window, right next to where Aaron was standing.

He squinted and peered into the backyard. The light was coming from the woods behind his house. He jumped when he heard a terrible screeching noise that sounded like a loud drill.

"I'll get back to you, Zoe," Aaron whispered, hanging up the phone. Now he knew something was really wrong.

Aaron called Adam. "Get over here quick! Everyone's menorahs are missing and something really weird is happening in the woods. I know it's getting dark, but bring your sunglasses. And I need your walkie-talkie too!"

"OK," Adam agreed. "But only for a minute. I don't want to miss getting my Hanukkah presents."

"Purr," called Aaron, "Where are you? I need your help."

"Don't bother me," Purr called back from the basement. "I'm trying to chase an ant!"

"Forget it," said Aaron. He grabbed his binoculars, sunglasses and walkie-talkie and headed out the back door.

CHAPTER THREE

IT'S A BIRD! IT'S A PLANE!
IT'S A LITTER BOX?

Adam was in Aaron's backyard in a minute.
"Wow!" he gasped. "I can't believe how bright
that thing is!" They put on their sunglasses and climbed
Aaron's double-decker tree house.

Aaron looked through the binoculars. He couldn't believe what he saw. There was a bunch of little furry creatures with big pointy ears. They were slightly smaller than a cat, slightly larger than a rat, with arms and legs just like people.

They were using a blowtorch and drills to attach upside-down menorahs to the bottom of a weird-looking object. It looked like a flying saucer, but it had a huge box on top. The box was full of little pebbles.

The invaders were making strange squeaky noises which sounded like they were talking to each other.

Aaron was so stunned, he couldn't speak.

Adam grabbed the binoculars. "What in the world?" he gulped, as an unpleasant odor made its way into his nostrils. "Is that a spaceship or a litter box?"

"Give me that thing," Aaron croaked, grabbing back the binoculars. "It looks like a humungous litter box. But I see a door in the side with a ladder leading to the ground. It must be a litter box spaceship!"

"Yuck!" They both shouted at once.

"Adam, take your walkie-talkie and sneak it over there so we can hear what they're saying," whispered Aaron.

"This is gonna be great!" Adam exclaimed. He jumped down from the tree house, held his nose and began to run on his tiptoes toward the spaceship.

After a few steps he got so scared by the bright lights and all the noise that he stopped in his tracks. But he took a deep breath through his mouth, gathered up his courage and continued to slowly sneak up as close as he dared.

~ ~ ~ ~ ~

CHAPTER FOUR
GIVE ME THAT MENORAH!

At that moment, Aaron heard a car drive into his driveway. It was his father, coming home from work.

"Perfect timing," thought Aaron. He jumped off the tree house and ran down to greet him.

"Dad! A bunch of little gray furry creatures stole everyone's hanukkiot and are using them to fix their spaceship in the woods behind our house. We need you to help us translate what they are saying!" Aaron was so excited that he could barely catch his breath.

"Sounds pretty crazy," yawned dad as he took his super laptop computer out of the car. "I'm exhausted. Can't you get your mother to help you? And what's all that noise about?" He was so tired from a long day at work that he hadn't completely realized what Aaron had said. He certainly didn't connect it with the racket coming from the backyard.

"But Dad! Mom is busy getting the Hanukkah presents ready. We can't interrupt her. Please!!" Aaron begged.

Before Dad had the chance to refuse, Aaron grabbed his arm and led him from the driveway to the backyard. When Dad looked into the woods, he finally realized that something bizarre really was happening. He climbed the tree house – which was no easy feat – and grabbed the binoculars.

"This is unbelievable! It looks like they are aliens whose spaceship broke and they are trying to use the menorahs as rockets to get back to their planet! And what's that smell?" he grimaced, fanning the odor away from his nose.

Just then, Adam ran back. "OK, I turned on my walkie-talkie. Turn yours on so we can hear what they're saying."

As soon as Aaron switched on his walkie-talkie, they heard a high squeaky voice shouting, "Me-ive me me-at me-ewdriver me-oh me-I me-an me-ix me-is me-ing."

"What?" Aaron, Dad and Adam all shouted at once. "What kind of language is that?"

"I'll power up my computer and see what I can find," Dad offered.

Just as he began to search his extraterrestrial sources, a squirrel ran by, followed closely by Purr.

"Huh? *Meowrats?*" Purr stopped in her tracks and cocked her head to one side. "I can't believe those *nincompoops* are here!

"I just heard on Cat TV that a meowrat spaceship from the planet *Catastrophia* made an emergency landing on earth because they were going out for milk and ran out of gas. All they need to do is get more fuel, but those numskulls think their rockets are broken.

"They're so dumb that they built their spaceship with a litter box on top so they wouldn't smell up the cabin when they needed to use the bathroom. It never occurred to those doofuses that they would have to walk out into space in order to use it! That's the stupidest…"

"Purr, stop calling them names! That's sooo not nice. Can't you just tell us what they're saying?" asked Aaron, flabbergasted.

"OK, OK," whined Purr. "One of them just told another one to give him a screwdriver so he could fix that thing. Everyone knows you can't fix a spaceship with a screwdriver. And the dumb thing isn't even broken!"

"Well, they obviously think they can use Hanukkah menorahs as rockets," Aaron suggested.

"Figures," said Purr, rolling her eyes, "Only a meowrat would think of something as bird-brained as that."

"What are we going to do?" asked Adam, beginning to get upset. "I need my menorah back or we won't be able to light the candles!"

CHAPTER FIVE

RABBI ROCKETPOWER TO THE RESCUE

At that moment, Rabbi Mensch walked down the stairs to the kitchen. "Aaron, where are you?" she called. "What's causing that terrible racket?"

"Oy! What's going on here?" she shouted, shielding her eyes from the beams of light as she stepped out of the kitchen door and into the backyard.

"Mom!" Aaron cried. He ran over and told her the whole story.

"I'll let you take it from here," moaned Dad as he hobbled past her into the house, dragging his computer. He tried to straighten his back after being hunched over the bench in the tree house for too long.

"I've got a plan," Rabbi Mensch told Aaron. "Get Purr to act as a decoy. You and Adam get ready to catch the menorahs. I'll take care of the rest."

Aaron knew what would happen next. His mother would transform herself into the courageous Rabbi Rocketpower... able to wipe out evil wherever she finds it, able to make bad guys turn good with a flick of her mighty yad, able to make peace where there is war with a single blast of her trusty shofar.

He saw her begin to spin faster than a dreidel. In a second, she was wearing her blue outfit with the big white star on the front and her tallis-like cape.

"Oy Vay! Up, up and away! Rabbi Rocketpower will save the day!" she shouted as she zoomed into the air.

"Quick," Aaron whispered to Purr, "go over there and distract the meowrats."

"What's in it for me, doughnut breath?" asked Purr, annoyed.

"I won't be able to give you the special present I got you if we can't light the Hanukkah menorah," Aaron warned.

"All right, all right," Purr grumbled. She walked into the woods and meowed in her most sugary, sweet voice, "Me-oo me-ants me-oo me-ay me-ing a-me-ound me me-osie?"

"I wish I knew what she was saying," sighed Adam.

"I figured it out!" Aaron beamed. "I think she said, 'Who wants to play Ring Around the Rosie?' "

"That's not going to work," moaned Adam. "They're not going to stop fixing their spaceship to play a children's game!"

But at that moment, they heard a lot of voices shouting, "Mee, mee, mee!"

"Then follow me, fur balls!" meowed Purr.

Aaron and Adam heard a loud rustling noise as a lot of little feet scurried after Purr to a neighbor's backyard.

While Purr tried to get the meowrats to stand in a circle and hold paws, and the boys stood waiting in the middle of the yard, Rabbi Rocketpower swooped down next to the spaceship. She filled the gas tank with a flick of her mighty yad, grabbed the menorahs and shot back up into the sky.

Suddenly Aaron and Adam heard a voice crying, "Look out below!" They looked up just in time to catch the menorahs of the eight Jewish families who lived on their street.

"Hooray! Our menorahs!" they cried. "Now we can celebrate Hanukkah!"

The meowrats heard the boys shout. They looked at each other and said, "Me-uh? Me-ut's me-at?" and ran screaming back into their spaceship.

"I didn't want to play with you hair brains anyway," Purr huffed as she stuck her nose in the air and pranced back to the house.

Adam grabbed his hanukkiah and ran home. Just as Aaron finished saying goodbye to his friend, he was nearly knocked to the ground by the tremendous roar of what sounded like an enormous car turning on its engine, followed by a blinding flash of light. He looked up just in time to see the spaceship shoot into the sky, leaving in its wake a huge trail of very stinky smoke.

"Yuck! That's so disgusting." Aaron grimaced, pinching his nose.

"Now that's what I call a Hanukkah candle," smiled Rabbi Mensch who suddenly appeared by his side. Aaron looked at her and realized that she also must have the super power to turn off her sense of smell.

CHAPTER SIX

A PURR-FECTLY HAPPY HANUKKAH

As Rabbi Mensch prepared the sufganiot and latkes and both Purr and Dad took much needed naps, Aaron returned the menorahs to their rightful owners.

He didn't quite know what to say when each family asked how he had ended up with their menorah. He figured that no one would believe that a bunch of aliens tried to use them as rockets for their spaceship.

A couple of people asked why their menorah seemed to be a little furry and smelled a bit like cat litter. He just shrugged and smiled.

Aaron ran home as quickly as he could so the Mensch family could light the candles on their menorah, say the blessings and exchange presents.

Aaron got a Rocketpower Junior outfit with a big blue 'A' on it. Dad got super-decoder software for his computer which Aaron noticed even included a language called "Meowratty."

Mom got a super light Torah commentary so she could study Torah while she was flying through the air on her missions.

Everyone waited anxiously to see what would happen when Purr opened her present. "Uch, what's this?" she complained as she clawed off the wrapping paper and saw a fishing rod and a rubber mouse. "I'm outta here."

But just as she was about to walk away, Aaron threw her the mouse at the end of the pole and began to reel it in. When she batted it away with her paw, it screamed, "Ouch! That hurt!" She grabbed the mouse, yanked the fishing rod out of Aaron's hand and ran into the other room. Everyone laughed as Purr yelled at the mouse.

After the family played dreidel, they sat down to eat their sufganiot for dessert. Suddenly Purr appeared and put her new mouse on an empty plate. "Well, I've got my dessert, bubs," she declared, victoriously. "Let's eat."

Rabbi Mensch chuckled, looked at her family and said, "Hanukkah is the holiday when we think about how our ancestors saved Judaism and the Temple in Jerusalem. We say, '*nays gadol haya sham* – a great miracle happened there' to give thanks for our ancestors' good fortune.

"This year, after saving the meowrats, returning everyone's hanukkiot and finding a toy which is finally up to Purr's high standards, we can truly say, as they say in Israel, '*nays gadol haya **poh*** – a great miracle happened **here**.' "

~ ~ ~ ~ ~

Purr's Purrfect Potato Pancakes (Latkes)

*Please do not attempt this at home unless there
is an adult there to help you.*

Ingredients

6 Russet or Idaho potatoes

3 large eggs

1 sweet onion

3 tsp. salt

1/2 cup flour or 3/4 cup matza meal

1 lemon

Canola oil

----

1. Peel and grate potatoes.

2. Squeeze out excess starch water.

3. Squeeze in lemon juice.

4. Peel and grate onion into mixture.

5. Beat eggs lightly and add to mixture.

6. Mix all together.

7. Pour enough canola oil into large frying pan to cover latkes.

8. Heat on stove medium/medium high.

9. Add latke mixture one tablespoon at a time.

10. Turn when the edges start to turn golden brown.

11. Cover a large plate with two paper towels.

12. When both sides are golden brown, remove and place on plate. Makes about 35 pancakes.

13. Serve immediately with either applesauce or sour cream.

14. YUM!!!

Rabbi Rocketpower's
Super Secret Sufganiyot
(Doughnuts for Hanukkah)

Please do not attempt this at home unless there is an adult there to help you.

Ingredients

1/2 cup warm water
2-1/2 tsp. yeast
1/4 cup granulated sugar
Salt
1 large egg, beaten
2 Tbsp. oil
1-1/2 cups all purpose flour
Canola oil for frying (3 inches deep)
Confectioners sugar
Jelly (optional – any flavor)

Mix 1/4 cup warm water with the yeast and 1 teaspoon sugar. When it foams, add the rest of the sugar, salt, egg, and 2 tablespoons oil. Put flour in a bowl and then pour the yeast mixture into the flour and combine well. Add another 1/4 cup warm water and combine. Cover with a damp towel. Allow it to rise for 1 hour.

Heat the oil in a heavy pot or deep fat fryer to 350°. If you don't have a thermometer, drop a little flour into the pot and if it sizzles, it's ready. Carefully put 1 tablespoon of dough into the hot oil. When the dough begins to slightly brown and puff up, remove it with a slotted spoon and place on paper towel to drain. After cooling, put the jelly into a pastry bag with a small round tip, and squirt the jelly into the middle of the sufganiot. Makes about one dozen.

Note: It is traditional to eat doughnuts and latkes on Hanukkah because they are fried in oil. It reminds us of the story of the little jar of oil the Jews found when they reclaimed the Temple in Jerusalem and how it miraculously lasted for eight days instead of one. It also adds to the fun of the holiday celebration.

Dreidel Game

Everyone sits in a circle (or a square, a triangle, a hexagon, a blob… anything with a middle).

Any number can play (except you need enough people to be able to make a middle between them). It gets boring really quickly if you are playing by yourself.

Each person starts with the same number of something to bet with (18 is a great number since it stands for "hai" which means "life" in Hebrew).

Rabbi Rocketpower prefers chocolate gelt. Aaron prefers any type of chocolate candy. Purr prefers catnip. Each person puts one or two pieces in the middle.

Then each one takes a turn spinning the dreidel. If it lands on the "nun," "nothing" happens. If it lands on the "gimmel," the spinner "gets" everything in the pot. If it lands on "hay," the spinner takes "half" of everything in the pot. If it lands on "shin," the spinner has to put a piece into the pot.

If you run out of pieces, you lose unless another player is a mensch and gives you some of their pieces. The game ends when everyone either gets tired or really hungry and eats their pieces (unless they are made of catnip).

Aaron suggests that you try spinning the dreidel upside down and see who can make it spin the longest.

Purr suggests that you give her all of your catnip so she can have a snack while she's watching Cat TV.

Glossary

Antiochus the 4th – Really mean Greek ruler who was the King of Syria and ruler of Palestine. He hated the Jews. He trashed their holy Temple in Jerusalem and tried to stop them from being Jewish. Don't worry. He lived over 2100 years ago.

Blintz – Tasty thin pancake rolled up with yummy ricotta cheese and/or fruity filling. Purr once ate a whole plateful of them, including a live one with cherry filling which didn't appreciate being in her stomach. Read the whole story in Rabbi Rocketpower's Blintzes Rule/Cats Drool, A Cheesy Tale for Shavuot.

Catastrophia – Planet of the meowrats. Not much happening there other than a bunch of broken down old spaceships. Rabbi Rocketpower, Aaron and Purr all agree that it's not worth the trip.

Dreidel – Top with four sides. Used to play a game on Hanukkah. Each side has one Hebrew letter which stands for a Hebrew word. The letter "Nun" stands for the word "nays" which means "miracle." The letter "Gimmel" stands for the word "gadol" which means "great" (as in really big). The letter "Hay" stands for the word "haya" which really means "was" but here it means "happened." The letter "Shin" stands for "sham" which means "there." Put it all together and you get "A Great Miracle Happened There." This refers to the miracle of how the Israelites defeated the Greek army and got back their holy Temple.

Gelt – Yum! Chocolate money wrapped in tin foil. The Yiddish word for "money." It reminds us of the money the Maccabees made when they got back their freedom.

Hanukkah – Literally means "rededication." The name of the Jewish holiday celebrating the Israelites' miraculous victory over the Greek army in ancient Israel.

Hanukkiah – A nine-branched menorah used on Hanukkah. The highest branch is for the "shamash" candle which is used to light the rest. The hanukkiah is lit each of the eight nights of Hanukkah. Each night, an additional candle is lit, signifying the number of days of Hanukkah which is being celebrated.

Kosher – Special Jewish dietary laws which include not eating pork products, shellfish, not mixing milk and meat at a meal, etc. When someone says something "is kosher," they means that "it's OK." Saying something is "not kosher" is another way to say "it's not OK." OK?

Latke – Yummy potato pancake fried in oil; as miraculous as the little jar of oil that burned for eight days after the Jews won back the Temple in Jerusalem. Don't eat too many or your tummy won't feel like celebrating.

Maccabee – The Hebrew word for "hammer." It refers to the brave Jews who fought the Greek army. A man named Judah, who lived with his family in Modiin, was called a "Maccabee" because he was as strong as a hammer.

When the Greek army came to their town and commanded that they bow down to Greek idols and give up their Jewish beliefs, Judah's father Mattathias refused. He, his five sons, and other Jews fled into the hills. Judah became the leader of the group after Mattathias. They began an army which eventually defeated the Greeks and took back the Temple in Jerusalem. "Maccabee" is also an abbreviation for a phrase from a Jewish prayer "Who is like You, O G-d, among the gods…"

Matzah Ball – Fluffy ball of dough made out of matzah meal. Rabbi Rocketpower prefers them when they're a little chewy. Ever tried matzah ball soup? It's delicious!

Menorah – Any candle holder which holds numerous candles. This word is often used to refer to a hanukkiah.

Mensch – Yiddish term for someone who is very nice, helps others and often does mitzvot (good deeds).

Meowrats – Inhabitants of the planet Catastrophia. Half cat, half rat. Guess which half is which.

Mitzvah – A good deed. Technically one of the commandments in the Torah.

Modiin – Hometown of the Maccabees. If you're ever in Israel driving from Tel Aviv to Jerusalem, stop by. Not only is it a cool place to visit, but the rabbi there is Rabbi Rocketpower's friend.

Nays Gadol Haya Poh – Hebrew phrase used in Israel meaning "A Great Miracle Happened Here." This is what the four letters on an Israeli dreidel stand for. Israelis say "poh" (here) instead of "sham" (there) since the miracle of Hanukkah happened in Israel.

Nays Gadol Haya Sham – Hebrew phrase meaning "A Great Miracle Happened There." This is what the four letters on a non-Israeli dreidel stand for.

Nincompoop – Very uncomplimentary expression used by Purr. You'd never catch Rabbi Rocketpower calling someone this. Hopefully, Aaron wouldn't either.

Oy Vay – O No! It's a little bit of a pain.

P.I.A – Short for "Pain In the Asteroid," Purr's home planet. Don't bother going. Everyone there is really annoying.

Rabbi – Teaches Jews and non-Jews about Judaism, leads worship services, gives advice, helps Jews celebrate important times in their lives. Very rewarding.

Shma Yisrael – Means "Hear O Israel" in English. The beginning of the most important Jewish prayer. If you are Jewish, hopefully you know the rest. If you don't, get someone to teach it to you. It reminds us that there is only one G-d.

Shofar – Ram's horn that Jews blow to announce the Jewish New Year (Rosh Hashanah) and the end of the Day of Atonement (Yom Kippur). Cooler than a siren. Try it sometime. Bet you can't make a sound come out of it.

Sufganiyot – Dough fried in oil. Ever had a doughnut? That's what these are. Very popular in Israel. Rabbi Rocketpower squirts jelly in the middle because that's the way Aaron likes them. Purr couldn't care less.

Sukkot – Eight-day holiday which comes right after Yom Kippur; major harvest pilgrimage festival when Jews thank G-d. It is like a Jewish Thanksgiving. Jews build little huts (Sukkot) where they can eat and sleep during the holiday. It's not just a coincidence that Sukkot and Hanukkah are the same number of days. Sukkot is the holiday the Jews actually celebrated when they rededicated the Temple.

Tallis – A prayer shawl which can be worn by adult Jews when they pray during the day. If you're leading a Jewish worship service, you wear one even if it's night. It really makes you feel special when you wear one, like you're being wrapped in Jewish tradition or being hugged by G-d. You can try one on to see how it feels even if you're not an adult. Try it, you'll like it. It also has really cool fringes tied in a bunch of different knots on each corner called tzitzit. Rabbi Rocketpower sometimes likes to wrap one of the tzitzit around her finger during the service. Look up tzitzit on the internet and learn all about it.

Torah – The Biblical story of the Jewish people, including 613 commandments for Jews to live by. Also called the Five Books of Moses. Can you name them? (Answer: Genesis, Exodus, Leviticus, Numbers, Deuteronomy)

Yad – You're not supposed to touch the Torah scroll with your fingers out of respect for its holiness. This is the name of the pointer you use so you won't lose your place. Means "hand" in Hebrew.

ACKNOWLEDGMENTS

This book would not have become a reality without the super powers of the Rabbi Rocketpower team.

The publication of this book became possible when Carol Feltman, long-time member of my congregation and Chief Administrative Officer of Oak Leaf Systems, agreed to be its publisher. She has generously spent innumerable hours making sure every last detail was accurate. She has made each step of this production a joy and as much fun as it could be.

Ariel DiOrio has blossomed into an incredible artist and illustrator right before our eyes! Even as a child, she would impress everyone in our temple with her drawings. Her creative approach to each illustration is a testament to her talent, intelligence and determination to perfect her craft and delight the readers of this book.

When Susanna Natti, published illustrator of numerous children's books and longstanding member of Temple Shalom Emeth, generously agreed to be our Artistic Director, I knew it would become worthy of publication. Susanna's wisdom, advice and encouragement have been invaluable to Ariel, Carol and me. Her positive energy has helped to make the whole process a blast!

Thank you to Lisa DiOrio and Martin Abeshaus for creating a terrific website, www.rabbirocketpower.com.

Thank you to Fran Landry and Rosalind Gordon for being our proofreaders.

Most of all, thank you to my son Aaron.

In the fall of 2001, when he was in the First Grade, the world seemed to him to be a particularly scary place. I began to evolve Rabbi Rocketpower stories with him to focus his attention on caring and positive role models. I also wanted to teach him about the Jewish holidays in a fun and funny way.

Our family became super heroes, saving Jewish holidays from those who threatened to keep us from enjoying them. We both thought it was important for there to be children's stories which featured a woman rabbi as both a mother and a super hero. This book would not exist without Aaron and his imagination, his intelligence, his perspective and his sense of humor.

Thank you to the students and teachers at the Rashi School and at Temple Shalom Emeth for their comments, suggestions and encouragement.

Thank you to all the members of Temple Shalom Emeth for their support.

Rabbi Susan Abramson, D.D.
September 2007

~ ~ ~ ~ ~

"ONE *MITZVAH* LEADS TO ANOTHER."
(Pirkei Avot Chapter 4, Mishnah 2)

Watch for these upcoming Rabbi Rocketpower Adventures:

A Tutti-Fruiti Tale for Tu Bishvat

A Purr-fectly Preposterous Purim

A Pharoah-cious Passover

Blintzes Rule/Cats Drool - A Cheesy Tale
    for Shavuot